MOTHS

By William Anthony

BUGS

KidHaven PUBLISHING

Published in 2022 by
KidHaven Publishing, an Imprint of Greenhaven Publishing, LLC
353 3rd Avenue
Suite 255
New York, NY 10010

© 2022 Booklife Publishing
This edition is published by arrangement with Booklife Publishing

All rights reserved. No part of this book may be reproduced in any form without permission in writing from the publisher, except by a reviewer.

Edited by: John Wood
Designed by: Amy Li

Find us on

Cataloging-in-Publication Data

Names: Anthony, William.
Title: Moths / William Anthony.
Description: New York : KidHaven Publishing, 2022. | Series: Bugs | Includes glossary and index.
Identifiers: ISBN 9781534537743 (pbk.) | ISBN 9781534537767 (library bound) | ISBN 9781534537750 (6 pack) | ISBN 9781534537774 (ebook)
Subjects: LCSH: Moths--Juvenile literature.
Classification: LCC QL544.2 W555 2022 | DDC 595.78--dc23

Printed in the United States of America

CPSIA compliance information: Batch #CSKH22: For further information contact Greenhaven Publishing LLC, New York, New York at 1-844-317-7404.

Please visit our website, www.greenhavenpublishing.com. For a free color catalog of all our high-quality books, call toll free 1-844-317-7404 or fax 1-844-317-7405.

PHOTO CREDITS – Images are courtesy of Shutterstock.com. With thanks to Getty Images, Thinkstock Photo and iStockphoto.
Cover – AR Pictures, Karramba Production, Ermak Oksana, ten43, azure1, Ortis, Cornel Constantin, Eric Isslee, Jiri Hodecek, Pixeljoy, Tomasz Klejdysz . Recurring Images – ten43, THPStock (paper), Cornel Constantin (header texture), kensson (main background), abeadex (vector moths in header), Karramba Productions (parchment), Andrey Eremin, Steve Paint (labels), azure1 (magnifying glass), Ortis, enterphoto, Le Do, grahixmania (page decoration), Ermak Oksana (doodles). P1 – AR Pictures, Pixeljoy, p2-3 – Forcus, p4-5 – StockImageFactory.com, Johannes, Kornelius, Eileen Kumpf (web), David Havel, p6-7 – Sandra Standbridge, meunierd, p8-9 – Brett Hondow, Matee Nuserm, p10-11 – Robert Garner, Andreas-H, p12-13 – Florian Teodor, Videostudia, p14-15 – MotionLight, apiguide, toey19863, 16-17 – Ed Reinsel, Les Weber, schankz, p18-19 – Ian Redding, Ben Sale (wiki commons), p20-21 – Dr Morley Read, jbmake, Dumbledore, Nathadech Suntarak, p22-23 – Vaclav Volrab, StockSmartStart, Mike McDonald, p24 – AR Pictures

CONTENTS

PAGE 4   Explorer Training
PAGE 6   What Is a Moth?
PAGE 8   Adaptations
PAGE 10 Home Life
PAGE 12 Life Cycle
PAGE 16 Finding a Feast
PAGE 18 Staying Safe
PAGE 20 Moth Madness
PAGE 22 Time to Explore
PAGE 24 Glossary and Index

Words that look like **THIS** can be found in the glossary on page 24.

EXPLORER TRAINING

Hey, over here! Do you want to be our newest bug expert? We have a team of explorers and it needs another member. You could be perfect for the job! First, we need to give you some training.

This book will teach you all about moths, those marvelous winged insects you've probably seen fluttering around your porch light at night. So grab your notepad and your magnifying glass, and get ready to fly high with these beautiful bugs!

WHAT IS A MOTH?

Before we start, we need to know about the different parts of a moth. Moths are a type of insect. Insects have no backbones and have six legs attached to their bodies.

The three main parts of an insect's body are the head, the thorax, and the abdomen.

Some moths have colorful patterns on their wings.

Antennae

Moths have a pair of antennae at the top of their heads, which help them to **SENSE** the world around them. Moths can also fly, thanks to a set of four wings.

ADAPTATIONS

Moths have **ADAPTED** to be able to do different things. Different moths have adapted to be awake at different times. Some are awake at night and some are awake in the day.

The pellucid hawk moth is a type of moth that is awake during the day.

Some scientists believe moths that are awake at night have adapted to follow the moon and stars. They follow these bright objects to help them find their way around.

Flannel moths are awake at night.

HOME LIFE

Moths live on every **CONTINENT** of our planet, except Antarctica. Some moths live in the warmth of Africa and South America. Others live in the freezing temperatures of the Arctic.

The moon moth can be found across the south of Africa.

Moths can be found in the tallest mountains and in the shortest grasses. Some moths even travel from country to country.

The crimson speckled moth flies to and from different countries, often in Europe.

LIFE CYCLE

Moths weren't always the winged creatures that you see in this book. They first start out as a little, round egg. Eggs are laid by female moths.

Some **SPECIES** of moths can lay up to 1,000 eggs at a time!

When the egg hatches, a caterpillar appears from inside. Caterpillars can be big or small, come in all sorts of colors and patterns, and can even be hairy. Caterpillars are the **LARVAL STAGE** of a moth.

13

When the caterpillar is old enough, it becomes a chrysalis. This is when a hard case forms around the caterpillar. Inside, the caterpillar is changing into something very different.

Caterpillars can form a chrysalis in many places, such as in fallen leaves or hanging from tree trunks.

When it's ready, the new insect will break out of the case. It's not a caterpillar anymore – it's a moth! Soon, the moth will fly away and start the process all over again.

15

FINDING A FEAST

Most adult moths don't eat at all. Instead of eating, they get everything they need by drinking. Moths will drink almost anything that **DISSOLVES** in water.

Their favorite meal is the **NECTAR** from flowers. To drink the wonderful nectar in the plant, moths use a proboscis, which is like a big straw.

STAYING SAFE

In the wild, moths have lots of **PREDATORS**. However, some moths have adapted to stay well hidden. Peppered moths can blend in with tree trunks and keep out of sight of other animals.

Can you spot all the moths on this tree?

The Chinese character moth has a different approach to hiding. It's colored to look like a bird's poop! This stops its predators from wanting to eat it.

MOTH MADNESS

Have you ever noticed that when you leave a light on at night, moths seem to fly around it? Scientists still haven't quite worked out why they do this.

Some scientists believe that moths mistake lights for the moon, and they use the lights to **NAVIGATE**. Others believe that male moths think the lights are females they can **MATE** with.

Why do you think moths might like lights?

TIME TO EXPLORE

Well, that's the end of your training. Good news – you've passed! You are now ready to go out and explore the wilderness, armed with your new knowledge. But there's one more thing you'll need before you go…

...your well-earned explorer's badge! Here it is, and it means you are now a moth expert. Why not make your own badge and wear it with pride? Congratulations, explorer!

GLOSSARY

adapt — to change over time to fit with the environment
continent — a very large area of land, such as Africa or Europe, often made up of many countries
dissolve — to become part of a liquid
larval stage — an early part of some animals' lives, when they look very different than their adult form
mate — to create young with an animal of the same species
navigate — to find a way around
nectar — a sweet liquid made by plants
predator — an animal that hunts other animals for food
sense — to feel or be aware of
species — a group of very similar animals or plants that are capable of producing more of their kind

INDEX

abdomen 6
antennae 7
caterpillars 13–15
chrysalises 14
day 8
eggs 12–13
head 6–7
legs 6
lights 9, 20–21
nectar 17
night 8–9, 20
proboscis 17
thorax 6
wings 7, 12